In the Moonlight, Waiting

by Carol Carrick

Illustrated by Donald Carrick

Clarion Books

New York

FOR DON

— C.C.

Clarion Books
a Houghton Mifflin Company imprint
215 Park Avenue South, New York, NY 10003
Text copyright © 1990 by Carol Carrick
Illustrations copyright © 1990 by The Estate of Donald Carrick

Library of Congress Cataloging-in-Publication Data

Carrick, Carol.
In the moonlight, waiting / by Carol Carrick : illustrated by
Donald Carrick. p.   cm.
Summary: In the spring during lambing time, a family wakes in
the middle of the night to welcome Clover the sheep's new baby.
ISBN 0-89919-867-8
[1. Sheep—Fiction.   2. Farm Life—Fiction.]   I. Carrick, Donald,
ill.   II. Title.

PZ7.C2344In   1990   89-17430
[E]—dc20   CIP   AC

HOR 10 9 8 7 6 5 4 3 2 1

A Note About the Illustrations

This book is illustrated with the watercolor sketches Donald Carrick made in preparation for the final paintings. Sad to say, he was not able to complete any of the paintings before his untimely death. However his wife, Carol, along with his editor and art director, decided that the sketches were so fresh and lively that they could not only serve as the illustrations, but also contribute a special poetry of their own.

Waking from a dream,
I hear footsteps
on the stairs.
The kitchen door opens
and shuts.

I shake Tim,
trembling with the cold
and with excitement.
"Hurry!" I say,
"Mom's already gone out."

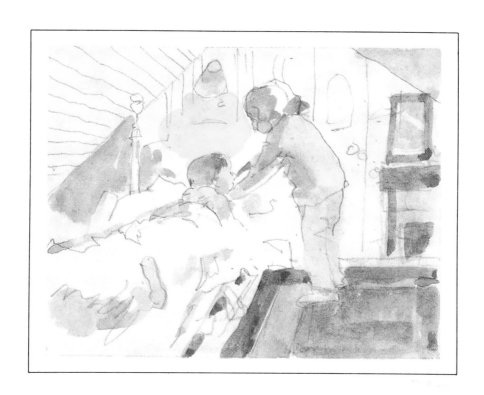

"Careful!
Don't wake Dad."

The stairs creak
all
   the
      way
        down.

"Hold still, please."
"But you put my boots
on the wrong feet!"

Duke greets us,
tail thumping.
His cold nose
shoves my hand.
"Where is she, Duke?"
"Where's Mom?"
Duke snorts
and rattles his chain.

The sheep watch us
at the fence,
jaws moving,
sides heaving.
Their ears turn
at a leaf
dancing in the wind.

A light winks
at the far side
of the pasture.
We slip through the fence
and the sheep run off.

"Over here," Mom calls.
"Clover has lambed."

The ewe
dries the lamb
with her tongue
and helps him to stand.
Anxious,
she circles him.

Mom lets me carry him
to the barn.
The lamb bleats
and the new mother
follows us,
bawling.

Star stretches
to nuzzle us.
We show him
our first lamb.

In the pen,
the lamb
wobbles to me,
collapses,
and struggles
to his feet.
He butts my knees.

"Look, Tim!
He thinks I'm his mother."

I bring him
to Clover
who sniffs him,
knowing her lamb
by his smell.
She washes
and feeds him,
and we leave them
curled up together,
safe and warm.

The sheep watch us
at the fence,
jaws moving,
sides heaving.
Their breath
hangs in clouds.

Flop-ear's bag
is heavy with milk.
She's ready to lamb,
Mom says.
"Tonight?" I ask.
"Maybe.
You never can tell."

Next to the kitchen stove,
Muffin lifts his head.
He circles the chair
and settles down.

Mom makes some tea
before she naps.
Dad will be up
at dawn.

Now
Tim is sleeping,
Mom is dozing,
and Dad sleeps on...

...while I watch
in the moonlight,
waiting for more lambs.